# Irene's Wish

To fathers

—J. N.

To all loving families of the world

—AG F.

SIMON & SCHUSTER BOOKS FOR YOUNG READERS
An imprint of Simon & Schuster Children's Publishing Division
1230 Avenue of the Americas, New York, New York 10020
Text copyright © 2014 by Jerdine Nolen
Illustrations copyright © 2014 by AG Ford

For information about special discounts for bulk purchases, please contact
Simon & Schuster Special Sales at 1-866-506-1949 or business@simonandschuster.com.
The Simon & Schuster Speakers Bureau can bring authors to your live event. For more information or to book an event,
contact the Simon & Schuster Speakers Bureau at 1-866-248-3049 or visit our website at www.simonspeakers.com.
Book design by Chloë Foglia and Krista Olsen • The text for this book is set in Cochin LT Std.
The illustrations for this book are rendered in acrylics and oil on illustration board.
Manufactured in China • 0814 SCP
2 4 6 8 10 9 7 5 3 1
Library of Congress Cataloging-in-Publication Data
Nolen, Jerdine.
Irene's wish / Jerdine Nolen ; illustrated by A. G. Ford.
pages cm
Summary: "From award-winning author Jerdine Nolen comes a tale of a little girl who wishes for her father to be home
more, but she never expects her wish to come true the way it does"—Provided by publisher.
ISBN 978-0-689-86300-4 (hardback) • ISBN 978-1-4424-9323-0 (eBook)
[1. Wishes—Fiction. 2. Fathers—Fiction. 3. African Americans—Fiction.] I. Ford, AG, illustrator. II. Title.
PZ7.N723Ir 2014
[E]—dc23
2014011622

# IRENE'S WISH

BY JERDINE NOLEN

ILLUSTRATED BY AG FORD

A PAULA WISEMAN BOOK
Simon & Schuster Books for Young Readers
New York  London  Toronto  Sydney  New Delhi

Things are back to normal now, but something happened last spring—well, my family will never be the same. It's Papa. You see, he makes things grow. People are always showing up at our front door with planters, potting soil, flowerpots, and seedlings. They all want one thing: to get my papa and his magic growing touch to make their plantings grow.

Papa's work keeps him quite busy. He's too busy to play with us. I wondered if there could be a time when he wouldn't be so busy—when he'd just stay home and play.

Papa always says, "If a star can grow inside an apple, *anything* is possible!" Then he cuts an apple crosswise and shows us the star inside. He removes the seeds, though. He tucks them inside his pockets. He never leaves *them* lying around. "Seeds," he says, "are *very full* of possibilities."

I believe in Papa. So I planted my own kind of seeds in hopes and dreams and wishes. I hoped and dreamed and wished on all the stars that sparkled in the skies and on all the apples that ever dangled from any tree. That's when all the trouble started.

My parents warned us not to eat or swallow seeds. "They'll *grow* inside you." Most folks chuckled at their warning. But Papa did not.

My brother Jimmy and I managed to stash a secret supply of seeds—big ones, just right for a spitting contest. So one day, when no one was looking, we would spit those seeds all the way to Timbuktu!

In the spring, Papa was working hard in the yard, so I brought him some iced tea.

Now when it came to iced tea, my papa was not a drinker or a sipper—he was a chug-a-lugger. Chug-a-lug, chug-a-lug. Chug-a-lug. He gulped every last drop of that ice-cold refreshing liquid and every last one of those seeds we had hidden in that cup. Papa knew something was wrong the minute he gulped the last drop. I believe folks heard him shouting clear down to the other side of Yonders Creek!

If I had only grabbed a different cup. If only I had not accidentally given Papa our secret seed supply. . . . But Mama says sometimes things happen just the way they happen.

That night and the next day, Papa lay around being sick. By the third day something was happening. He looked all green around the edges of his face. Mama tried to comfort him, but he could not be comforted.

He wanted sunlight. Mama had us take down all the curtains in the room. He wanted air. Mama had us open all the windows. He needed water—gallons and gallons of water. Papa drank a lot of it. But he asked us to pour most of it on and around him. In the end, I thought he would burst or just float away.

You should have seen the look on our faces when we realized that our seeds were germinating inside Papa's stomach.

When it appeared our house could no longer hold him, we moved Papa to the center of everything. That way he would always be a part of our home . . . and yard. That's when I realized my wish had come true—only not the way I'd thought it would!

Now when people came to our house, they came mainly to inquire about Papa. They brought the morning paper and sat in his shade and read to him. Or they came to bring the news of the neighborhood or talk about the good growing season.

Mostly they came to see how he was doing. They complimented him on how well he was filling out and offered to prune him.

When my friends Donna, Shelby, and Nick came over, we played hide-and-seek in and around his roots and branches. And those times he would laugh and laugh, right along with us, but he never gave our hiding places away. In May we tied pretty ribbons to his arms (which stuck out like branches), and we danced around him, singing.

At night Mama would sit with him. She'd sing to him
or they just talked. I know they missed each other. Papa
couldn't dance or snuggle or talk as easily as before. And we
all knew he was homesick for the old days.

We took some of his favorite things outside to keep him
company. After all, we were still a loving family. Whether
your papa is a tree or a man, you still love him. But I worried
day and night about my wish and how I could unwish it.

As spring grew into summer, my papa grew bigger and stronger and wider. He thrived in the sun. Mama prepared most of our meals outdoors, and we ate them sitting in his shade. We even made a game out of watering Papa.

He looked so strong and mighty, like an oak. We were not quite sure what kind of tree he was turning out to be, so we just called him Papa-Tree. We all wanted Papa back the way he used to be, but I did not want things back to "normal." I did miss Papa, his hugs, and his soft voice. And I knew I needed to unwish my wish.

Colder winds came with autumn. Trees began to shiver and shake and change the color of their leaves. But none of them dazzled and sparkled in the full flames and colors as my papa did out in the autumn sun. He was spectacular. Even after all the trees had shed their leaves, Papa kept all of his. Papa was always one to do things in his own way. We all felt proud. Throughout the fall he was the most beautiful tree.

The first winter morning Papa dropped his last leaf. It drifted to the ground like the falling and wandering snow. That night our neighbors sat vigil with us. They worried, too, about the coming storm.

That was one night I wished and hoped and dreamed again with all my heart and all my might on all the apples and on all the stars: "Please," I spoke out quietly to the night. "Please let us have our papa back again."

When we awoke the next morning, the earth was blanketed in white. Our Papa-Tree was not there. But our papa was. There on the ground he was sleeping, snoring loudly.

Papa woke up stretching. He said he had a big long dream he was trying to remember.

We took him in by the fire. He said he was glad to be warm and awake, surrounded by his family. He said he felt like he had been very silent and very still for a long, long time.

When it was my turn to talk, I knew I had to tell Papa everything: about our seeds accidentally getting into his iced tea, about my hoping and wishing and wanting him to be home with us, about all the things we'd done together and all the fun we'd had. I told him about the home he'd given to birds and squirrels. And . . . I told him *exactly how* I unwished my wish.

Papa sat very still and silent. "All in all," he said, clearing his throat, "swallowing seeds wasn't the worst thing in the world. It turned out to be a good thing. It's like I always say: 'If a star can grow inside an apple, *anything* is possible!'

"Wishes and seeds are alike," Papa told us. "They are full of possibilities. All the while you're planting your seeds—or while you're making up your wishes—you have to get ready for a time when your wish will come out just right. Prepare to live with what you wished for!"

I knew exactly what Papa meant.

"Possibilities are all around us," Papa said. "I believe it just may be possible for me to save some time to be with Mama and Jimmy and Baby Thomas . . . and you, Irene, who made this wish for us all."